THE SORRY LIFE OF TIMOTHY SHMOE

For Shmoe (aka Trysten), and for Sarah and Eryn — S.S.M.

For my husband, Kevin — Z.S.

Owlkids Books acknowledges the financial support of the Canada Council for the Arts, the Ontario Arts Council, the Government of Canada through the Canada Book Fund (CBF) and the Government of Ontario through the Ontario Creates Book Initiative for our publishing activities.

Published in Canada by
Owlkids Books Inc.
1 Eglinton Avenue East
Toronto, ON M4P 3A1

Published in the United States by
Owlkids Books Inc.
1700 Fourth Street
Berkeley, CA 94710

Library and Archives Canada Cataloguing in Publication
Title: The sorry life of Timothy Shmoe / written by Stephanie Simpson McLellan ; illustrated by Zoe Si.
Names: McLellan, Stephanie Simpson, author. | Si, Zoe, illustrator.
Identifiers: Canadiana 20200275186 | ISBN 9781771473934 (hardcover)
Classification: LCC PS8575.L457 S67 2021 | DDC jC813/.6—dc23

Library of Congress Control Number: 2020940653

Edited by Karen Li and Katherine Dearlove
Designed by Diane Robertson

Manufactured in Guangdong Province, Dongguan City, China, in October 2020, by Toppan Leefung Packaging & Printing (Dongguan) Co., Ltd.
Job #BAYDC82

A   B   C   D   E   F

 ONTARIO ARTS COUNCIL
CONSEIL DES ARTS DE L'ONTARIO
an Ontario government agency
un organisme du gouvernement de l'Ontario

Canada Council
for the Arts

Conseil des Arts
du Canada

Canadä

 Publisher of Chirp, Chickadee and OWL
www.owlkidsbooks.com | Owlkids Books is a division of  bayard canada

THE SORRY LIFE OF TIMOTHY SHMOE

Written by Stephanie Simpson McLellan

Illustrated by Zoe Si

Owlkids Books

Timothy Shmoe was not a bad kid . . .
But sometimes he did bad things.

Sometimes he made honest mistakes.

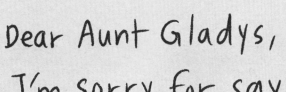

Dear Aunt Gladys,

I'm sorry for saying I didn't like the sweater you knit for my birthday. I said that because Dad says I must always tell the truth.

I guess he isn't telling the truth about that.

Sincerely sorry,
Your nephew, Timothy

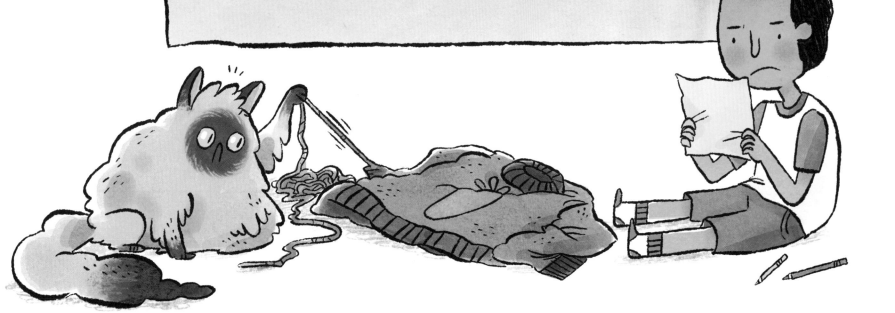

Sometimes, to be honest, he knew exactly what he was doing.

Sometimes things
were broken.

Dear Dad,

I'm sorry my slapshot knocked your great-great-grandma's vase off the shelf.

(Who knew I could shoot so high?!)

Sincerely sorry,
    Your loving son, Timothy

P.S.: That vase was pretty old-looking anyway, don't you think?

Other times, things were just . . . changed.

Timothy's sisters were occasionally guilty of planting ideas.

But mostly, he was surrounded by innocent bystanders.

Dear Great-Nanny Gough,

I'm sorry you got trapped in the corner when Mom went to buy milk. In my defense, no one told me our house is a little crooked.
I didn't know your wheelchair would roll so fast after I released the brakes.
Now I know that when you scream like that, it means you are scared and not excited.

Your GREAT-grandson,
Timothy Shmoe

Even though Timothy found himself in trouble a lot ...

Dear Fluffy,

I pulled your tail because you scratched me.

I am ^not really sorry.

From, Timothy

P.S.: I know that you can't read this, so I don't know why Dad made me write it.

… his apologies were (mostly) sincere.

Dear Fluffy,

Dad said I needed to try this note again. He reminded me that I am bigger than you and that cats are not horses.

Now I know that when you screech like that, it means you are scared and not ~~exited~~ excited.

From your human,
Timothy Shmoe

And his mistakes usually had small consequences …

… until they multiplied.

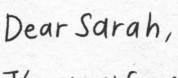

Dear Sarah,

I'm sorry for shooting marbles across the floor of your ballet show.

I was trying to copy those things you were doing with your arms and forgot about the marbles in my hands.

Sincerely sorry,
Your brother, Timothy

Dear Eryn,

I'm sorry for shooting marbles across the floor of your ballet show. I jumped on the stage to help, but now I know you should NEVER pick a dancer up by the tutu because the material is VERY fragile.

Sincerely sorry,
Your brother, Timothy

Timothy's parents were frequently frazzled.

Dear Miss Shirley,

I'm sorry for shooting marbles across the floor of your ballet show. I now know that:

1) People in the audience should STAY in the audience.

2) Bringing marbles to a dance show is NOT a good idea.

3) You should NEVER lift a dancer by the tutu.

Thank you for teaching me these important lessons and sincerely sorry again.

Sarah and Eryn's very sorry brother,
          Timothy Shmoe

P.S.: I'm missing my really cool red Mars marble, and I wonder if maybe you have it?

But one thing was for sure.
No matter what Timothy did or how often he did it . . .

His family loved him just the same.

DEAR TIMOTHY,

THERE IS NOTHING YOU COULD DO
THAT WOULD MAKE ME NOT LOVE YOU.

I WOULD ONLY BE SORRY IF YOU WERE
NOT MY SON.

YOUR EVER-LOVING DAD
XOXOXOXOXOXOXOXO

P.S.: CAN'T WAIT TO SEE WHAT
YOU'VE DONE!